MY 1ST
GRAPHIC
NOVEL

LILY'S
LUCKY
LEOTARD

My First Graphic Novels are published by Stone Arch Books,
A Capstone Imprint
1710 Roe Crest Drive
North Mankato, Minnesota 56003
www.capstonepub.com

Library of Congress Cataloging-in-Publication Data
Mortensen, Lori, 1955-
    Lily's Lucky Leotard / by Cari Meister; illustrated by Jannie Ho.
    p. cm. — (My first graphic novel)
    ISBN 978-1-4342-1296-2 (library binding)
    ISBN 978-1-4342-1411-9 (pbk.)
    1. Graphic novels. [1. Graphic novels. 2. Gymnastics—Fiction.]
I. Sullivan, Mary, 1958- ill. II. Title.
PZ7.7.M45Li 2009
741.5'973—dc22   2008031964

Summary: Lily practices gymnastics every day. She even has a new leotard.
Now she needs to land the star jump on the balance beam. Find out if her
lucky leotard will help her land the star jump.

Art Director: Heather Kindseth
Graphic Designer: Hilary Wacholz

Printed in the United States of America.
012017   10233R

LILY'S LUCKY LEOTARD

by Cari Meister

illustrated by Jannie Ho

STONE ARCH BOOKS
www.stonearchbooks.com

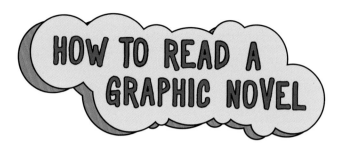

HOW TO READ A GRAPHIC NOVEL

Graphic novels are easy to read. Boxes called panels show you how to follow the story. Look at the panels from left to right and top to bottom.

Read the word boxes and word balloons from left to right as well. Don't forget the sound and action words in the pictures.

The pictures and the words work together to tell the whole story.

Lily ran up the steps.

She pushed open the gym door.

She was in the locker room.

Lily opened her bag and smiled.

My new lucky leotard!

ZZZZIP

There it was! Her new leotard.

Lily ran to the mat.

She felt great in her new leotard!

Today, she was going to do it.

Today, she was going to make the star jump on the balance beam.

Coach Punch wanted his gymnasts to work hard.

"You have to push yourself," he said,
"If you want to be the best."

Lily wanted to be the best.

First the gymnasts warmed up.

They stretched.

They ran laps.

They hopped.

They jumped.

Next they practiced floor exercises.

They stood tall.

They pointed their toes.

They flipped over and over and over.

Then they practiced the vault.

Lily stuck her landing.

Coach Punch was very proud.

That was great!

Yes!

Lily's new leotard was bringing her luck.

Finally it was time for the balance beam. Lily had been practicing the star jump for weeks.

A star jump took skill and balance.

Lily mounted the beam. She took a deep breath. She pushed off.

She made a great star. But she did not land right.

"You almost have it," said Coach.

Lily jumped on the beam.

She took a deep breath.

22

She pushed off.

She made a great star.

JUMP!

Then Lily landed. She put up her arms and smiled.

Lily completed the perfect star jump!

Lily and her lucky leotard were a great match!

ABOUT THE AUTHOR

Cari Meister is the author of many books for children, including the My Pony Jack series and *Luther's Halloween*. She lives on a small farm in Minnesota with her husband, four sons, three horses, one dog, and one cat. Cari enjoys running, snowshoeing, horseback riding, and yoga. She loves to visit libraries and schools.

ABOUT THE ILLUSTRATOR

Born in Hong Kong and raised in Philadelphia, Jannie Ho studied illustration at Parsons School of Design in New York. Jannie has been drawing ever since she can remember. Much of Jannie's work and style has been inspired by Japanese and retro art.

GLOSSARY

balance beam (BAL-uhnss beem)—a long wooden beam that gymnasts perform on

cartwheel (KART-weel)—a sideways flip with arms and legs straight out

floor exercise (flor EK-sur-size)—a gymnastic event that focuses on tumbling and flips

leotard (LEE-uh-tard)—a tight, one-piece item of clothing

mount (mount)—a move used to get on a piece of gymnastics equipment

vault (vawlt)—a small padded table that gymnastics flip over

DISCUSSION QUESTIONS

1.) Lily's leotard was her good luck charm. Do you have any good luck charms? If so, what are they?

2.) Lily practiced her star jump a lot before she got it right. She never gave up. What is something that you've worked extra hard at?

3.) Coach Punch knew Lily could do the star jump. He believed in her. Name a person who believes in you. Explain what they do to show you they care.

WRITING PROMPTS

1.) During their warm-up routine, the kids stretched, ran, and jumped. Pretend you were the coach. Write down at least five things you would do for a warm-up.

2.) Lily's new leotard brought her luck. Draw a picture of something that brings you luck.

3.) Throughout the book, there are sound and action words next to some of the art. Pick at least two of those words. Then write your own sentences using those words.

THE FIRST STEP INTO GRAPHIC NOVELS

My FIRST Graphic Novel

These books are the perfect introduction to the world of safe, appealing graphic novels. Each story uses familiar topics, repeating patterns, and core vocabulary words appropriate for a beginning reader. Combine the entertaining story with comic book panels, exciting action elements, and bright colors and a safe graphic novel is born.

WHAM!

MY 1ST GRAPHIC NOVEL

GOALKEEPER GOOF

by Cori Meister
Illustrated by Cori Doerrfeld

MY 1ST GRAPHIC NOVEL

THE END ZONE

by Lori Mortensen
Illustrated by Mary Sullivan

RAH-RAH RUBY!

by Christianne C. Jones
Illustrated by Cori Doerrfeld

T-BALL TROUBLE

by Cori Meister
Illustrated by Jannie Ho